Stock and Rocket

Published in 2023
First published in the UK by Stock and Rocket
An imprint of Igloo Books Ltd
Cottage Farm, NN6 0BJ, UK
Owned by Bonnier Books
Sveavägen 56, Stockholm, Sweden
www.igloobooks.com

0223 006
6 8 10 9 7 5
ISBN 978-1-78905-829-1

Written by Stephanie Moss
Illustrated by Jacqui Davis

Cover designed by Bethany Dowling
Interiors designed by Kerri-Ann Hulme
Edited by Stephanie Moss

Printed and manufactured in China

This book belongs to:

....

Stock and Rocket

Fairy Ballerina

The fairies were excited for the disco in Fairyland,
but why they were so happy, one fairy couldn't understand.

Twinkletoes wasn't excited. She knew her dancing was really bad.
So she sat down on a toadstool, feeling nervous and quite sad.

Fairyland
Disco

"You just need to be brave," Fairy Crystabelle would say.
"We'll show you what to do, so you're ready on the day."

The fairies turned on the music and danced along to the beat.
They showed Twinkletoes how to twirl and tap her little feet.

On the night of the disco, Twinkletoes still wasn't prepared.
"Don't worry," said her friends. "There's no need to be scared!"

The fairies set off to the disco at Sparkle Lake.
They reassured their friend she wouldn't make a mistake.

When they got to the disco, everything twinkled with fairy light.
Suddenly, Fairy Twinkletoes couldn't wait to dance all night!

Twinkletoes danced and pranced. She swirled and twirled.
The little fairy knew she had the best friends in the world.

Dress-Up Fairy

Fairy Crystabelle couldn't wait to go to the magical Fairyland Ball,
but when she looked inside her wardrobe, she had nothing to wear at all.

"What am I going to do?" poor Fairy Crystabelle cried.
She'd never have time to make a new dress, however hard she tried.

"Don't worry," said her friends. "Everything will be fine.
We can make you a beautiful ballgown that is sure to shimmer and shine."

So they fluttered their shiny wings and went into the fairy wood,
to find as many things for her new dress as they possibly could.

They found toadstools, leaves and petals lying on the ground.
They took out their magic wands and swished them all around.

Crystabelle's new dress looked better than she could have dreamed.
It shimmered with fairy dust and jewels that glittered and gleamed.

When Crystabelle arrived at the ball, everyone began to stare.
All her lovely friends thought she was the prettiest fairy there.

"I'm so pleased," said Crystabelle, "that we made my dress together."
Then she twirled around and said, "You are the best friends ever!"